Sixty
Thousand
Sisters

Daughters of the Queen

*To Marishka –
Life is such a
wonderful adventure!
C Tal*

Written by Christine Tailer

**with photographs by
Christine Kuhr
Monica Kohler
Christine Tailer**

With special thanks to the honey bees.

First Printing: Winter 2015

ISBN 978-1-312-82496-6

Published by:
Straight Creek Valley Farm Publishing
6489 Straight Creek Road
Georgetown, Ohio 4521
www.straightcreekvalleyfarm.com

Ordering Information:
Special discounts may be available with quantity purchases by corporations, associations, educators, and others.
For details, please contact the publisher at the above address.

(cover photo by Monica Kohler)

Sixty Thousand Sisters
Daughters of the Queen

The beekeeper's apiary sat at the edge of the upper field, not too far from the cabin.

It was springtime in the creek valley, and the bees had begun to fly across the fields in search of pollen and nectar.

Photo by Monica Kohler

Deep inside each of the beekeeper's hives, the new bees were just beginning to climb from their cells and meet the rest of their sisters.

There was one bee in particular that was beginning to feel a bit cramped inside her somewhat larger cell. She knew that it was time for her to eat her way through the capped wax wall by her head and greet the rest of the bees in the hive.

She was the new Queen.

Photo by Christine Tailer

Her attendants stayed close by her side as she made her way down through the hive to the entrance.

She stepped out into the sunshine, stretched her wings, and flew, for the first and only time, unless the hive swarmed ... but then that is another story.

Photo by Christine Tailer

The Queen bee circled higher and higher into the clear blue sky as a warm breeze carried her scent to the male bees, the drones, who rushed to greet her.

This one flight might be the only one that she would ever know, so she flew for as long as she could, high over the creek valley where the bee hive stood.

When the Queen returned to the hive, she was greeted by her waiting attendants.

They all marched inside, and the Queen began to lay eggs, carefully depositing one egg at the bottom of each of the six sided cells in the hive's brood chamber.

Photo by Christine Tailer

All through the summer the Queen would lay as many as two thousand eggs in a single day.

And all through the summer the beekeeper would keep a watchful eye on the Queen and her hive.

Photo by Christine Kuhr

After only twenty one days, as spring grew outside, the first of the newly laid eggs had grown up into a young worker bee, daughter of the new Queen.

The young bee stayed in the hive's brood chamber, tending her newly laid sister eggs, and feeding the growing larvae.

Then, when she was about two weeks old, the young bee began to collect the wax that had begun to grow like scales on the underside of her abdomen.

She used the scales to build the hive's six sided wax comb.

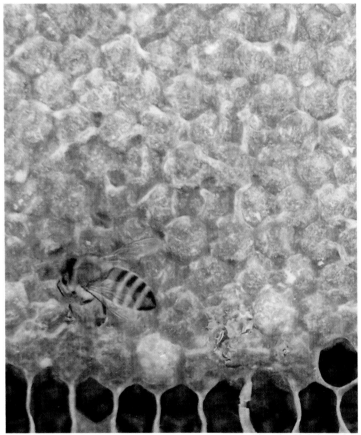

Photo by Christine Kuhr

The young bee's older sisters, daughters of the former Queen, had already learned to fly, and were bringing pollen and nectar back to the hive.

Photo by Monica Kohler

In time, when the young bee was about four weeks old, she too was ready to leave the hive.

Photo by Monica Kohler

Older bees danced at the hive entrance, signaling the young bee where to find the best blossoms.

Photo by Christine Tailer

After a few practice flights she headed out, following her sisters' directions.

She flew out across the fields and landed on a sweet smelling flower.

Photo by Monica Kohler

She sucked the flower's nectar through her straw like tongue into a special nectar stomach.

11

Other honey bees, and even two bumble bees, gathered pollen and nectar from the flower beside her.

Photo by Monica Kohler

Photo by Monica Kohler

The bees stuffed the pollen into sacks at the back of their hind legs, and as they flew from blossom to blossom, they brought pollen from one flower to another.

Without a doubt ...

Photo by Christine Tailer

... the bees loved the lavender colored basil that grew in the beekeeper's garden.

And then at dusk, all of the bees returned to the hive.

Photo by Christine Tailer

A group of sister bees stood at the hive entrance fanning their wings backwards, sending the hive's scent out onto the summer breeze and signaling the colony's stragglers that it was time to return home.

Photo by Christine Tailer

The guard bees touched the returning bees and would not allow any strange scented outsiders to pass through. Only their sisters could enter.

The young bee went straight to the hive's upper chamber, passing off her full load of nectar to an even younger bee who deposited the gathered nectar into a comb cell.

Photo by Christine Kuhr

Other bees fanned their wings to draw moisture off the nectar and turn it into honey.

Still other bees capped the honeycomb's six sided cells with a protective layer of wax.

And all through the summer days and nights the Queen worked, laying thousands and thousands of eggs.

Photo by Christine Kuhr

The beekeeper continued her careful watch and listened to the hive's contented hum.

She crouched safely off to the side of the hive, out of the bees' flight path, and they did not even know that she was there.

Soon there were sixty thousand sister bees, all living together and working together in the hive.

Photo by Christine Kuhr

There were nursery bees, wax making bees, and guard bees.

Some bees cleaned debris from the hive.

The body brigade removed any dead bees by pushing them down to the hive entrance and rolling them out to the grass below.

And then the days began to grow shorter.

The sisters banned their brother drones from the hive.

The guard bees would not let the drones enter, because there was no reason for the sisters to feed their hungry brothers all through the winter.

The brother bees tried and tried to get past the guards at the hive entrance, but the guards kept pushing them back, and eventually the drones gave up, and went away.

Photo by Christine Tailer

Without the warmth and honey of the hive, the lonely drones soon died.

By the time the first snow fell, the sister bees no longer left the hive and the Queen was not laying any eggs at all.

Photo by Christine Tailer

The bees all huddled together in a cluster in the central chamber, surrounding the Queen, and moving ever so slowly. The heat generated by their movement kept the Queen warm.

And as the winter winds blew up and down the creek valley, the bees ate their stored honey. The Queen's attendants carefully fed her, and stayed close beside her.

Months passed and the Queen stayed safe and still in the center of the cluster. She did not start to move about and lay eggs again until warm weather had returned, and her daughters began to fly again and bring pollen and nectar back to the hive.

The seasons came...

Photo by Christine Tailer

... and went.

First one, and then a second year passed.

And then it was spring again, and the garden began to grow.

Photo by Christine Tailer

And the bees began to fly...

... but the Queen was an old queen now.

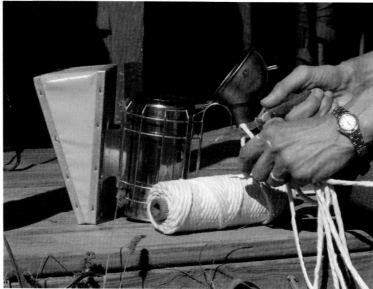

She no longer lay her eggs in a neat pattern.

She rather lay them scattered throughout the hive, and her scent was not quite right.

Both her daughters and the beekeeper knew that something was wrong.

There was a difference in the sound of the bees' buzzing, and their flights away from the hive grew erratic.

Finally, the old Queen was barely laying any eggs at all.

Photo by Christine Kuhr

The beekeeper was worried, and continued her close watch, but finally she was able to smile.

A few of the Queen's attendants had chosen a healthy, newly laid egg that was low in the hive.

After three days, when the chosen larva hatched from its egg, the nursery bees fed her a special mixture of food ...

... and as the larva ate, she grew larger than her sisters.

Five days later, the attendants capped the end of her cell, and as the new Queen grew, the old Queen grew weaker and soon died.

Photo by Christine Kuhr

The body brigade rolled out the old Queen's body without any ceremony at all.

The hive was now queenless.

The bees signaled their distress by the high pitch of their buzz and the confusion of their flights, but after only sixteen days the new Queen had grown and her cell had become very cramped.

Photo by Christine Kuhr

It was time for her to eat her way through the capped wall by her head and meet the rest of the bees in her colony.

Photo by Christine Kuhr

As she emerged from the cramped cell, her scent passed from bee to bee, and a contented buzz sounded throughout the hive.

Photo by Christine Kuhr

She was the new Queen.

The End.

(but as you know ...
    it is really just the beginning)

Christine Tailer was born and raised in New York City, where she spent much of her childhood looking up between the tall buildings to find the sky. After raising her children in Cincinnati, she and her husband moved to a 63 acre, off-grid farm in southern Ohio, where Christine now practices law part time, raises goats, meat rabbits, and chickens, tends a large garden, and of course, cares for her bee colonies, with whom she has fallen completely in love. You can visit Christine on the web at *straightcreekvalleyfarm.com*.

Monica Kohler recently took a hiatus from her nurse practitioner career to pursue her love of photography and travel from her home in Cincinnati to where ever her heart and family may lead her. She enjoys going on adventures with her children and grandchildren and always has her camera, and its many lenses, close at hand. Her creative eye draws her primarily to natural, sunlit settings with botanicals, which is where she is frequently joined by bees. You can reach Monica by e-mail at *monica@monicakohler.com* or see more of her work on line at *monicakohlerphotography.com*.

Christine Kuhr grew up in Cincinnati, Ohio, where she developed her career as a fine artist specializing in painting and photography. As a child she reached for and conquered every coloring book she could get her hands on, not really understanding why her mother told her not to step on the bees. Now, through working with her friend Christine on the *Sixty Thousands Sisters*, she has learned to appreciate the mighty role bees play in life, and is thankful for her mother's wisdom. You can find Christine on the web at *christinekuhr.com*.